The Little Lost Mermaid

Written by Lori M. Loughney
Illustrations by Cynthia I. Bonsant

Portland, Oregon

Copyright © 2021 Lori M. Loughney

Illustrations by Cynthia I. Bonsant

ISBN: 978-1-63304-035-9
First Printing: 2021

Cover & Interior Art: Cynthia I. Bonsant
Editing: Minnesota Minions, Unltd.
Copyediting: Claudia Kuzmanich
Book Design & Cover: Lorelei

Portland, Oregon
www.TrainWreckXPress.com
2021

For Samantha

because she asked for
a story about a Mermaid

Once there was a mermaid who lived under the sea.

She was loving and caring,

but she had no family.

She tried very hard to keep herself busy but she often felt sad, lonely and dizzy.

She wanted to start a rock 'n' roll band

3

But the dolphins
and sea stars didn't
have any hands.

4

She thought to teach dance
out on the coral reef,
but the salmon and seahorses
didn't have any feet.

5

She wondered each day if
she'd ever had a name.

She made up so many
it became a strange game.

6

She dreamed of a chance to study at school . . .

. . .but couldn't escape the waves and ocean pool.

So she sat on some seaweed and admired her flipper . . .

. . . and wished that her outfit had come with a zipper.

8

Then one day noises growled overhead.

"Is it a shark?" she cried and wished she'd stayed in bed.

She swam up to
the surface at a
comfortable range.

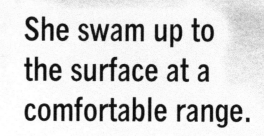

She saw something
odd-shaped and
definitely strange.

She floated in
the water and
saw a big
boat.

On the deck were two
girls in bright blue
and green coats.

11

The girl in the blue coat was familiar it seemed.

Though the mermaid felt scared, she said, "Hi, look at me!"

The mermaid watched the girl lean over the side to look down in amazement and gasp, "Oh, my!"

The one dressed in blue was joined at the rail by a green-coated girl with a long ponytail.

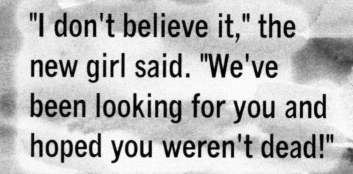

"I don't believe it," the new girl said. "We've been looking for you and hoped you weren't dead!"

"We knew we would find you if we didn't give in."

"So we never stopped looking for our sister with fins."

16

"I don't understand,"
the tiny mermaid said.

"Because when you
left us you were out
of your head."

"Are you definitely sure
that I'm who you think?"

This is yours!" and she held
up a coat of bright pink.

"Sam?" the green girl said,
a quaver in her voice.
"If that's you, then it's time
you must make the big choice."

"What do you mean?"
the mermaid asked, all upset.

"You have to pick dry land
or stay permanently wet."

The mermaid closed her eyes and remembered her past. She *did* have a family, they'd found her at last!

She started to cry, she was trapped in the sea.

No way to go home and be with her family.

19

Kicking with her flipper, she was sad but afloat, then a strange thing happened as she looked at the boat.

Her tail started tingling, her scales went cold,

she felt her bottom half suddenly unfold.

20

Something snaky and white zinged past her head.
She grabbed at a rope and preserver and said,
"I choose dry land, I'm done with the sea!
Being a mermaid's not all it's cracked up to be."

21

They pulled her to the boat
as her tail fell away.
She skimmed across the water
with legs weak and gray.

The girls worked together
to get her up to the boat.
They got her out of the water
and wrapped in the pink coat.

They brought her
eight crumpets
with butter and hot tea.

They rubbed lotion on her legs and dried her completely.

She shivered and shuddered, her teeth chattered away.

Now she was near them, she didn't know what to say.

25

Tina was the name of the girl dressed in blue.
Smart and the oldest with a singing voice, too.

The girl in the green ~ AJ was her name. She was strong and wise and good at sports and games.

Of course, Sam was the youngest of all the three.
She had no idea how she'd got lost at sea.

"Let's find our parents!"
AJ said with a shout.

Tina said, "They'll
be so glad that
we got Sam out."

They set sail for their home
far away to the northwest,
feeling lucky and brave as
they finished their Quest.

But sometimes
at night Sam
missed life
in the water.

She secretly
dreamed she
was still the
Ocean's
daughter.

29

She swam with the dolphins

and sang with the whales.

She played tag in the seaweed

and flipped her mermaid tail.

She was powerful,
sleek, and filled with
love and care.

31

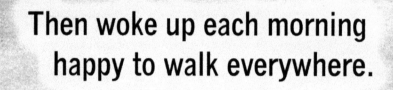

Then woke up each morning
happy to walk everywhere.

The End

Acknowledgments

My niece Samantha was seven years old when she asked her scribbler of an aunt for a mermaid story, which she received a few days later. But a decade passed since then, and only now is the rest of the world seeing *The Lost Little Mermaid*. The gorgeous artwork, created by my sister, Cynthia Bonsant, has been waiting a long time for its unveiling.

Cynthia always gives profound thanks and gratitude to God and to her wonderful family: Tom, Joshua, Emily, and Matthew. We are grateful for our siblings: Vince, Jeannie, Debbie, Angela, and Rob. Thanks also go to Claudia Kuzmanich for her eagle-eye editing and to the Minnesota Minions: Jessie Chandler, Judy Kerr, and MB Panichi for their encouragement for this project. Love to Lee Lynch, too, for always being the best fairy godmother a writer could ever wish for.

Much appreciation goes to Jeannie Loughney DePinto and her hubby Joe who welcomed me to be part of their children's lives, thereby ensuring a never-ending supply of humor, amazement, teen drama, and more than a few great characters and novel plots. Without children of my own, my nieces and nephews gave me the chance to have a taste of what it's like to be a parent – and then I could always return them when they were cranky or filthy or ran out of gas. I figure I got the very best of parenting experiences (without many expenses, or bath soap, or disciplining). The kids have been the greatest delight of my life.

Our dad, Frank Loughney, has been a source of inspiration and support, both when we were children and now that we're adults. Cynthia and I have such gratitude and appreciation for him, who we've been lucky to have in our lives much longer than most people get to enjoy a parent.

Big Love to Family!

Lori Loughney
Gresham, Oregon
November 2021

9 781633 040359